go girl

DISCARDS

Secret's Out

Secret's Out
first published in 2008
this edition published in 2013 by
Hardie Grant Egmont
Ground Floor, Building 1, 658 Church Street
Richmond, Victoria 3121, Australia
www.hardiegrantegmont.com.au

A CiP record for this title is available from the National Library of Australia

Text copyright © 2008 Chrissie Perry
Illustration and design copyright © 2013 Hardie Grant Egmont

Illustration by Aki Fukuoka
Design by Michelle Mackintosh
Text design and typesetting by Ektavo

Printed in Australia by Griffin Press, an Accredited ISO AS/NZS
14001:2004 Environmental Management System printer.

3 5 7 9 10 8 6 4

The paper this book is printed on is certified against the
Forest Stewardship Council® Standards. Griffin Press holds
FSC chain of custody certification SGS-COC-005088. FSC
promotes environmentally responsible, socially beneficial
and economically viable management of the world's forests

Secret's Out

by
Chrissie Perry

Illustrations by
Aki Fukuoka

hardie grant EGMONT

Chapter One

The hallway was noisy and busy, like it always was on Friday afternoons. It looked like a crazy jumble of arms and legs. Everyone seemed to be in a big rush to start the weekend.

Casey ducked in next to Tamsin and tugged her schoolbag down from its peg.

'Have you got everything?' Casey asked.

Tamsin nodded happily. Her parents were going away for the weekend, and so she was staying with Casey.

'I've got my pyjamas, my toothbrush ... and my dookie,' Tamsin giggled.

Casey smiled back. Tamsin was funny about her dookie. At Nina's birthday sleepover, Tamsin had taken a piece of red velvet to bed with her and rubbed it against her nose as she fell asleep.

It was one of those things Casey would have been embarrassed about. But the good thing about Tamsin was that she totally didn't care if her friends knew.

'Look what else I've got,' Tamsin whispered. 'A midnight snack.'

Out of her bag, from underneath the pyjamas, came a giant bag of mixed lollies.

'Oh, not fair!' Ivy exclaimed from across the hall. She screwed up her nose. 'I wish I could come!'

Casey smiled at her apologetically. 'Sorry, Ives,' she said. 'I really did try, but Mum said that one extra person for two nights was enough.'

Casey and Tamsin quickly ducked as a very mouldy apple flew past them.

'It's a goal!' yelled Dylan Moltby, throwing his arms in the air as the apple landed in the rubbish bin.

'Ewww!' Tamsin groaned. 'How long was *that* in your bag?'

Dylan grinned. 'Months, I think. Maybe years,' he said proudly.

Casey hid her grin as Dylan ran off.

'So, are you guys going to eat *all* of those lollies by yourselves?' asked Nina, who was now standing beside the girls, looking at the lolly packet. 'Or would you be kind enough to save some red snakes for me?'

'And will you save me some yellows?' Ivy added. 'Pretty please?'

'Red and yellow snakes will be totally untouched and ready for you guys,' Tamsin declared with a smile.

Casey waved goodbye as Ivy and Nina walked off. As she looked across at Tamsin, Casey felt a little shiver of excitement.

Casey wouldn't have said anything, but she was sort of glad she wasn't allowed to have Ivy and Nina over as well.

Even though Tamsin wasn't really new at their school anymore, it was still exciting to be around her.

At the beginning, everybody had wanted to hang out with Tamsin — except for Casey. It had been kind of hard watching a new girl march right into her group of friends, so Casey hadn't been very nice to Tamsin.

Maybe she would have handled it better if things had been OK at home. But Tamsin had arrived at school when Casey's parents were fighting a lot.

Casey had felt like everything in her life was changing, and all she wanted was for things to stay the same.

Casey felt a bit bad as she remembered how she had totally ignored Tamsin. Ivy and Nina were friendlier, and had got to know Tamsin really quickly.

After a while, Casey had realised that Tamsin was funny and nice. But there were still lots of things she didn't know about her, even though now they were in a club together with Nina and Ivy. The club was called the Secret Sisters.

It was completely different with Ivy and Nina. Casey had known those girls since they were all little. She knew them inside out. She knew their favourite colours and their favourite food, their favourite books and their favourite music.

'Oh, I brought my Taylor Swift CD,' Tamsin said, interrupting Casey's thoughts. She was fishing around in her schoolbag again. 'Do you like her, Case?'

Casey nodded. She'd just been thinking about music, and it was almost like Tamsin had read her mind. And Taylor Swift was, like, her second-favourite singer ever!

Casey grinned to herself as she and Tamsin walked down the corridor together and out into the warm afternoon sunshine. She giggled as Tamsin tossed the lolly bag into the air and caught it behind her back.

This weekend is going to be so fun, Casey thought happily. By Sunday, she and Tamsin would know everything about each other.

Then Casey's tummy did a funny little flip. *Maybe,* she thought, *just maybe, I'll even tell Tamsin my special secret.*

Chapter Two

'Let's turn it up again,' Casey said, reaching for the volume on the CD player.

Tamsin put her hands over her ears. Between the girls' music and the thumping rock tunes coming from Aaron's bedroom, the noise was pretty full-on.

'Turn it down!' The door to Casey's bedroom swung open, and her brother stomped inside.

'Hey, you can't do that!' Casey yelled.

But Aaron had already pushed the pause button.

'You are such a dweeb!' Casey said. 'You get to play your music all the time.'

Aaron is so annoying!

'Yeah, but *my* music is good!' Aaron said. He stood between Casey and the CD player, his arms folded.

'Hang on, so is ours,' Tamsin piped up. 'How about *we* get half an hour of our music, and then you can have half an hour of yours?'

Casey looked from Tamsin to Aaron. To Casey's surprise, Aaron seemed to be considering the deal.

'Ummm . . . nup,' he said finally.

'Then how about we get a whole hour, and we do something for you?' Tamsin went on. 'One of your jobs, maybe?'

'Yeah, like we'll set the table for you tonight,' Casey said.

Aaron looked as though he was weakening. '*And* I get to choose what TV we watch after dinner,' he bargained.

'OK,' Casey and Tamsin chimed in together.

Aaron walked out, looking very smug and satisfied.

'Hey, good work!' Casey whispered. 'Especially since it was *my* turn to set the table tonight!'

Tamsin burst out laughing. 'Brothers!'

Casey shook her head as she turned the CD player back on. It was great fun to dance around her bedroom with Tamsin. It was even better to find someone who knew what it was like to have a big brother.

Ivy had a sister and Nina was an only child. They didn't know anything about brothers. But Tamsin totally understood.

It looked like she and Tamsin had even more in common than Casey had hoped.

'Can you believe the noise Aaron made with his pappadums?' Casey said in bed that night, pulling her doona up under her chin.

'He was truly disgusting,' Tamsin giggled. 'But not quite as disgusting as Julian. My brother actually *drinks* his peas! He puts them on his tongue, gets a glass of water and swallows them down whole. It's gross.'

Casey turned onto her tummy and looked down at Tamsin, who was lying on the trundle bed.

It's so nice having a friend sleep over, thought Casey. Especially a friend who understood her life so well.

'Would you swap Aaron for a big sister?' Tamsin asked, stifling a big yawn.

Casey thought for a moment. It was a good question. Aaron could be a real pain. But then again, when she was having trouble with her maths homework, Aaron was the one who always helped her work out the problems.

And they had the best fun doing Warrior Wrestling matches. They made up silly names like Buster Strong-Heart and Lady Muck ... and Lady Muck was getting pretty good at getting Buster into a headlock!

'No,' Casey said finally. 'I actually wouldn't swap.'

Tamsin sighed sleepily. 'Me neither,' she said softly.

Casey put her arms behind her head and stared up at the ceiling. She felt really close to Tamsin at the moment. She felt like she could really talk to her.

Casey took a deep breath. Tamsin was definitely the right person to tell her special secret to.

It was something she hadn't told a single person, and it had been sitting inside her for at least two weeks!

'Tam?' she whispered, leaning over the side of the bed.

But Tamsin didn't say anything. Casey smiled to herself when she caught sight of the dookie lying on the pillow beside Tamsin's head.

Oh well, she thought, snuggling back under her doona. *Luckily we've got the whole weekend together. I can tell her tomorrow.*

Chapter Three

Casey normally got dragged to watch Aaron's soccer games on Saturday mornings. She would sit in the car for a while doing the kids' crossword in the newspaper. Then she would get a hot dog. Then she would wait a bit longer before getting a lemonade.

The idea was to stretch out everything good about going to soccer for as long as she could. But even with this plan, Saturday mornings were usually pretty boring.

Today was different, though. Casey and Tamsin were having the best fun in the playground next to the soccer field, mucking around in the old boat.

'OK, let's make it that I've got the treasure and you have to try and tap my shoulder three times before I hand it over,' Casey suggested.

'Yeah,' Tamsin agreed. 'And let's . . .' she trailed off, looking over Casey's shoulder at something. 'Hey!' called Tamsin, giving a little wave.

Casey looked in the direction of the wave. Ben Maddison, who went to their school, was walking over to them. He was staring at his feet as though his runners were the most interesting thing in the world. In fact, he hardly glanced up until he arrived at the boat.

'Hey, Ben. Are you watching someone play?' Tamsin asked.

Ben nodded, inspecting the boat's flaking paint. 'My brother,' he mumbled.

'Oh, which one is he?' said Tamsin.

Ben pointed awkwardly at a tall, lanky boy on the field.

Casey sat back in the boat and watched as Tamsin chatted to Ben. Tamsin was good at it, and she didn't seem to get shy. After a minute, Ben seemed less shy, too.

In fact, Casey noticed with a smile, soon Ben and Tamsin were laughing at one of the soccer players who'd taken a major dive in the dirt.

Eventually, Ben said goodbye and jogged back to the soccer field.

'He's cute, don't you think?' Tamsin asked thoughtfully. 'I think I might like him a bit, you know?'

'Really?' Casey asked.

Suddenly, her heart was thumping. Tamsin had told her something pretty special. And even though Casey had planned on telling Tamsin her own secret later on that night, before they went to sleep, it felt like now was the right time.

'Ah, Tamsin?' she said, but she sounded a bit croaky. She cleared her throat. 'Ah, Tamsin?' she repeated.

'Yeah?'

'I, er … I like Dylan Moltby.'

It felt strange to say it out loud. That secret had been stuck inside her for ages.

Casey had kept it totally to herself while Dylan stood around at lunchtime, telling jokes that made everyone laugh. And she kept it to herself when she sat behind Dylan in assembly.

Casey hadn't told anyone. Not Ivy. Not Nina. Not *anyone.*

So Casey had imagined Tamsin's jaw dropping in surprise when she told her. But it wasn't quite like that.

'Oh, yeah,' Tamsin said, nodding. 'Dylan Moltby is really nice. I mean, he's funny and stuff.'

Suddenly, Tamsin got a sneaky look on her face. She reached over and swatted Casey's shoulder three times.

'Hand over the treasure!' she demanded with a giggle.

Casey tried to duck, but it was too late. 'Hey,' she laughed. 'I wasn't ready!'

Tamsin had already scrambled away with the imaginary treasure.

'All right,' Casey yelled. 'I am *so* going to get you!'

The rest of the day was just as much fun as the start. But it went way too quickly, not like an ordinary weekend at all.

That night, the girls turned the lights off and climbed into bed. It was kind of naughty to clean your teeth, and then go to bed with a giant packet of lollies!

'Don't rustle the packet too much or Mum will come in,' Casey warned.

Tamsin grinned at her. 'Turn on the torch so I can see what I'm doing,' Tamsin whispered, popping another lolly in her mouth.

Casey turned the torch on, and Tamsin tipped all the lollies out of the bag. She carefully separated the red and yellow snakes, and put them into a little plastic bag they'd pinched out of the kitchen drawers.

'Do you think Ivy and Nina would know if we just ate one each?' Tamsin asked cheekily.

Casey shook her head. 'Not if we don't tell them,' she whispered.

After they'd eaten lots of lollies, Casey's

teeth felt all sugary. She thought about getting up and brushing them, but her eyelids felt heavy and tired.

Casey looked down at Tamsin in the torchlight, and saw her nicking another red snake. There weren't that many left in the bag, actually. If Casey had the energy, she would have told Tamsin to stop.

But another part of her didn't mind.
Casey could keep a secret.

And so could Tamsin. Couldn't she?

Chapter Four

Going to school on a Monday could be hard. But coming back on a Monday to an Italian-themed lunch was excellent! Casey loved it when school was like this.

Mrs Massola, their Italian teacher, had done a really good job. There was a big trestle table set up in the playground. Steam rose up into the air from huge pots filled with pasta and bolognaise sauce.

Casey waved at her friends from behind the trestle table. She'd been chosen to help serve the food.

'OK, guys,' said Mrs Massola, 'when everybody lines up, you put a serve of pasta like this, and then a scoop of sauce.'

The first kids in line were Holly and Olivia from Mr Mack's class. Casey grinned and chatted as she scooped pasta into their bowls. She was having fun serving up. Even though her mouth was watering and she would have to wait until the end to eat!

Soon, the line was really long. It seemed to Casey that there were a gazillion mouths to feed. She had to speed up. After a while, she barely noticed who she was serving.

Until Dylan Moltby was standing in front of her. Suddenly, Casey's hands felt a little bit shaky. She got the pasta in the bowl, but only half of the sauce made it onto the pasta. The rest landed on the ground.

Casey grabbed a fresh bowl, her face burning, and started all over again.

Casey was sort of glad when Dylan took his bowl of pasta and walked off. She felt like her face was as red as the pasta sauce!

Next in line were her besties. Casey grinned at them.

'Hey, can I have heaps of pasta and just a little bit of sauce?' Nina asked.

'And I'll just have a giant helping of everything,' Ivy added. 'Like the serve you gave *Dylan*.'

Casey froze. Then she stared at her friends. She saw Tamsin give Ivy a little nudge in the ribs.

It was so *obvious*. Casey dropped the ladle into the pot, and glared at Tamsin.

Tamsin had *told*. Casey's secret was out!

After Casey had finished serving up the pasta, she took her bowl and marched over to the courtyard, away from everybody. She was furious.

She sat down, watching the cloud of steam as it drifted up from her bowl. For a moment, Casey imagined that the steam was coming from her ears, like it does in cartoons when someone is cross.

Everyone else had finished eating, but suddenly Casey didn't feel hungry at all.

She could hear the little kids squealing from the playground. She could hear a ball thumping along the court. They were the sounds of a regular lunchtime. But it didn't feel regular to Casey.

'Hey, Casey. Are you OK?' said a voice.

Casey looked up as Tamsin sat down beside her.

Nina and Ivy stood in front of them.

'I can't believe you told my secret,' Casey said, looking at her shoes.

'That you like Dylan?' asked Tamsin. 'Um, yeah.'

Casey turned and glared at Tamsin.

Tamsin shrugged. 'Oops,' she said, like it was no big deal. 'I didn't mean to do anything wrong. It's just that we were all talking about boys we like, and ... well ...' she trailed off.

'Hey, you guys,' called Ching Ching from across the courtyard. 'The littlies want us to play chasey with them. Who's in?'

She pointed to a bunch of little kids who had their hands together, begging the older girls to join their game.

'That could be fun,' Tamsin said softly, looking at Casey.

Casey crossed her arms tightly. It was *so* annoying the way Tamsin just expected everything to go back to normal.

Casey felt a wave of anger rushing through her. Before she had a chance to think, she opened her mouth and let it all pour out.

'Yeah, you *should* play with the babies,' she said furiously. 'Since you're a baby yourself with that stupid dookie you have to rub against your nose to get to sleep.'

Suddenly, everything went quiet.

Chapter Five

'That,' said Ivy, with her hands on her hips, 'was really, really mean, Casey!'

Casey stared down at her bowl of cold spaghetti bolognaise. She pushed it around with her plastic fork.

She could hear Ching Ching and Holly chasing the little kids. She could hear lots of giggling as they caught a little girl with long plaits. And she could hear Tamsin clearing her throat, as though she was trying not to cry.

Now that those terrible words had come out of her mouth, Casey had absolutely nothing left to say.

Oh dear!

'Hang on,' said Nina, 'maybe Casey *was* a bit mean there. But Tamsin was pretty mean, too. If someone tells you a secret, you're not supposed to tell other people.'

'But Casey liking Dylan isn't really a secret,' Ivy protested. 'You all know who I like, and that's not such a big deal, is it?'

'No,' Nina said, 'but you don't *mind* that everyone knows who you like. If Casey didn't want anyone to know who she likes, then Tamsin shouldn't have told! And stop rolling your eyes, Ivy. It's really rude!'

It was like a ping-pong game, but with words instead of a little white ball. Ivy kept sticking up for Tamsin. Nina kept sticking up for Casey.

It was seriously weird how Tamsin hadn't said a word, and neither had Casey.

Casey sneaked a look at Tamsin. But Tamsin's head seemed to be stuck in her hands, and she didn't look up.

Suddenly Ivy grabbed Tamsin's hand and pulled her up to standing. 'Come on, Tamsin,' she said. 'Let's go and play by *ourselves*.'

The rest of the day was awful. Every time Casey thought about what she'd said to Tamsin, she felt sick to her stomach.

Whenever Casey tried to steal a glance at Tamsin, Tamsin would look away.

Whenever she tried to look at Ivy, Ivy stared back with her eyebrows raised.

During maths class, the problems on the sheet seemed impossible. Casey wasn't sure whether to add, subtract, multiply or divide.

I can't believe I said that to Tamsin.

Later, when they were supposed to be writing a diary entry about the Italian lunch, Casey's page stayed completely blank. She kept on imagining how good it would be if she could just write down the horrible thing she had said in pencil, and then rub it out. As though she could totally erase what she'd said from everybody's memory.

'Come on, Casey, get writing,' Mrs Withers said, standing behind her.

Casey nodded. She put her pencil to the page and started writing. Mrs Withers was right. She just had to get on with it.

Casey wrote about what it was like to serve out all that food. She wrote about the long queue, and chatting with Holly and Olivia. She even wrote about spilling Dylan's bolognaise sauce on the ground.

But as she was writing, Casey was thinking more about the things that she was leaving out of her diary entry than the things she was putting in there.

There was no way she could write about what had happened with Tamsin after she'd finished serving. It was confusing enough just thinking about it.

It was so upsetting that Tamsin had told the others her secret. A part of Casey still felt cross about it. But she also felt cross with herself. Really, really cross. She hadn't even meant to say that horrible thing to Tamsin. She actually thought Tamsin's dookie was kind of cute.

Casey felt like she and her friends were on a kind of see-saw. On one side, there was Tamsin telling everyone Casey's secret. On the other side, there was Casey being mean to Tamsin. And it was like Ivy had jumped onto Tamsin's end, and Nina had jumped onto Casey's.

Casey bit her lip. *How are we ever going to get off this see-saw?*

Chapter Six

'Hey, Case, how about some old-fashioned popcorn?' her mum asked, when Casey walked into the kitchen after school.

'What do you mean?' asked Casey quietly, taking the school newsletter out of her bag and putting it on the bench.

'You know, the kind that you make with oil in a saucepan, not in the microwave,' her mum said, raising an eyebrow. 'The kind you love, remember? Want some?'

Casey shrugged. 'I don't know.'

She sat on one of the bar stools on the other side of the counter. There was a lever underneath the seat that made it go up and down. Casey pulled it. She went up and down, up and down.

'You don't know whether you want *popcorn*?' her mum asked. She leant over the kitchen bench and put her hand on Casey's forehead.

'No fever,' her mum joked. 'So, what else could put my lovely daughter off popcorn?'

Casey could tell that her mum was waiting for her to crack a smile. But Casey just didn't feel like there was a smile inside her at the moment.

Her mum came around and sat on the bar stool next to Casey. She slyly reached under the stool for the lever, and started going up and down. But her timing was pretty bad.

When Casey rose up, her mum went down. When Casey went down, her mum rose up.

Actually, it was pretty funny. Casey tried hard not to smile, but in the end, after about twenty ups and downs, she couldn't help it.

'Hey, that's better,' her mum said. 'Can we please stop now? I'm getting dizzy.'

Finally, Casey and her mum were level with each other.

'What's wrong, sweetie?' her mum asked. This time, there was no joke in her voice. She sounded concerned.

'I had a really bad day.' Casey's voice crumbled as she spoke. But once she'd started, everything that had happened just tumbled out of her mouth.

She told her mum about liking Dylan. She told her mum about Tamsin telling everyone her secret. Then, and this was the hardest bit, she told her mum what she'd said to Tamsin about her dookie.

Casey's mum listened carefully.

'So, now,' Casey finished, 'I don't know what to do. Like, who's right and who's wrong?'

Casey's mum looked thoughtful. 'Maybe you're both right, and you're both wrong,' she said.

It was nice, sitting next to her mum, just talking.

'I was really upset when I found out that Tamsin had told the others about Dylan,' said Casey. 'I really just wanted it to be private. Don't you think it was mean for her to tell?'

'Did you ask Tamsin to keep it a secret?' her mum asked.

'Well, maybe not exactly,' Casey said. 'But it's obvious isn't it? Like, how am I supposed to be friends with someone I can't even trust?'

Casey's mum shook her head. 'Maybe it wasn't obvious to Tamsin,' she said. 'And you did trust all those girls when things were a bit rough here at home, didn't you? They were all pretty terrific then. Didn't they help you a lot, Case?'

Casey thought hard for a moment. Her mum was right. All of the Secret Sisters, Ivy, Nina, Tamsin and Casey, had taken turns helping each other.

Casey had to admit that they were the best friends when her mum and dad were fighting a lot. In fact, Casey wondered how she ever would have got through that time without them.

'I guess the thing is,' her mum went on, 'friends make mistakes. Even grown-up friends can make mistakes. Even parents make mistakes! Sometimes you have to try really hard to work things out.'

Casey nodded thoughtfully. And then she had an idea. Suddenly, Casey felt a little better. Actually, she felt absolutely starving.

'How about some of that old-fashioned popcorn, Mum?' she asked with a smile.

Chapter Seven

The next morning before school, Casey spent ages on the computer making pretty invitations. She put daisies all around the border, just like the daisies that decorated Tamsin's peg at school.

When she was finished, she printed out three invitations. Her heart fluttered as the pages came out of the printer.

TO THE SECRET SISTERS
You are invited to an
emergency meeting!
Place: Casey's cubby
Time: 4.30pm TODAY!

Aaron poked his head into the study.

'What are you doing up so early?' he asked, rubbing his eyes. 'And what are you printing? It woke me up, dweebarama.'

'Well, dweebarooma,' Casey replied, tucking the invitations into her schoolbag, 'I had something important to do.'

'Well, dweebarooni,' Aaron said, getting a little bag out of the pocket of his pyjamas and popping something red in his mouth, 'it was lucky you woke me up so early. You gave me heaps of time to find your stash!'

'Aaron!' Casey exclaimed. 'We were saving those for Nina and Ivy!'

Aaron grinned cheekily, popping a yellow snake in his mouth.

'Finders keepers!' he teased, waving the bag around. Then he narrowed his eyes. 'Unless,' he said dramatically, 'Lady Muck would like to wrestle me for the snakey prize?'

Casey rolled her eyes, but inside she was kind of glad. Warrior Wrestling was a great way to let off steam. And, even though she felt good about her plan to solve the argument between her friends, part of her still felt knotted up with worry about how the meeting would go.

Casey was already planning some good wrestling moves as she jogged out to the Warrior Wrestling trampoline.

Aaron beat her outside and jumped up to bounce-jog on the tramp, yelling in his loud commentator voice.

'Today, we have Lady Muck and Buster Strong-Heart fighting for the Red and Yellow Snakes Title,' he bellowed, using his hand as a microphone. 'Will Lady Muck be able to shake off last week's sad, bad performance to take the title? Or will Buster Strong-Heart be king yet again?'

Casey jumped up onto the trampoline, transforming herself into Lady Muck. She edged her way around the sides, doing little jumps and growling at Buster. He bounced around, punching the air with his fists.

Buster was pretty tricky. While Lady Muck was watching Buster's hands, Buster kicked out his leg, flipping Lady Muck behind the knees. Her legs buckled.

'And Lady Muck looks set to go down!' Buster yelled.

But Lady Muck recovered. She steadied her feet and rose up to standing position. She held her arm out and dived behind

Buster. And then Lady Muck sprung her famous headlock over his shoulder.

'One, two, three – ten!' she shouted. 'Lady Muck is the champion wrestler of the world. Hand over the loot, Buster Weak-Heart!'

Buster wriggled out of the headlock. Then he jumped off the trampoline and ran inside the house, giggling madly.

'Aaron!' Casey groaned. 'I won! And those lollies are for Ivy and Nina!'

Casey climbed off the tramp and followed her brother inside. She would have liked to dob on him, but she knew that Warrior Wrestling wasn't exactly popular with their parents, especially first thing on a school morning. Dobbing on Aaron would be dobbing on herself.

Brothers!

Casey rolled her eyes when she saw Aaron darting towards his bedroom.

She knew that once he went in there, there was absolutely no chance of her finding the lollies. Aaron's bedroom was like a rubbish tip!

Never mind, thought Casey, heading into the kitchen and pouring herself a bowl of cereal. *I've got more important things to worry about than red and yellow snakes. Like the emergency meeting at four-thirty this afternoon!*

Chapter Eight

That afternoon, Casey was pacing around her cubby house, looking at the photos on the wall. She paused in front of the one of her with Justin Bieber.

Tamsin's brother had cut and pasted pictures of the Secret Sisters with their very own star. If you looked closely you could tell the photos weren't real.

But Casey liked them anyway, and they made the cubby house look cool.

Casey sighed. She wanted things to go back to the way they were before.

School that day had been a bit better than yesterday. No-one had mentioned the argument, which was good, but also bad. Because even though the Secret Sisters had all played together with the girls from Mr Mack's class, it was obvious that something was still wrong.

Things weren't totally horrible any-more, but Casey felt like she and her best friends weren't as close as they had been before the argument. It used to feel like the four girls were linked together, like the links in a chain. Now, it felt like some of those links were about to snap.

Casey flopped into a beanbag. She picked up one of her favourite magazines and started flipping through the pages.

She caught sight of a picture of Taylor Swift, and remembered how she'd felt on Friday afternoon when Tamsin had asked if she liked her.

Casey sighed again. Friday afternoon seemed like a long time ago now.

Casey turned the page. In the centre spread, where staples held the magazine together, was a quiz called, *What sort of friend are you?*

Casey scanned the questions quickly. *Perhaps we can start the meeting by doing the friendship quiz together*, she thought, feeling a little happier. This was the sort of quiz they all loved. *Well, the sort of quiz we used to love . . .*

Casey's thoughts were interrupted by car doors slamming in her driveway.

Casey's tummy lurched a little as she peeked through the cubby house window. Ivy and Tamsin had arrived together!

It shouldn't have been such a surprise. Ivy and Tamsin lived in the same street, so it made sense for them to share a lift. Casey just felt a bit nervous that she would be there alone with them before Nina arrived.

'Hi, Tamsin! Hi, Ives!' Casey tried to keep her voice sounding bright. But it still wobbled a little bit.

Ivy walked through the cubby door in front of Tamsin, her arms crossed firmly.

'Well?' Ivy said.

Tamsin stood quietly next to Ivy.

Casey scratched her head. 'Well, what?'

'Well, you can say sorry to Tamsin now,'
Ivy said bluntly.

Casey took a deep breath, and tried not to feel upset all over again.

'Hang on,' said Nina, suddenly appearing in the cubby house doorway. 'How about Tamsin says sorry first, since she's the one who did the wrong thing first?'

Nina walked over to Casey and stood next to her.

Casey closed her eyes. Nina and Ivy were at it all over again! This definitely wasn't working out the way she'd planned.

Tamsin took a sideways step, away from the protection of Ivy.

'I'm sorry, Casey,' Tamsin whispered.

For a moment, Casey wasn't sure whether she'd heard right over the noise of Ivy and Nina arguing. But then Tamsin continued.

'Case, I honestly didn't think . . . I still don't really understand why you liking Dylan was such a big secret. But I promise I didn't mean to betray your trust.'

Casey smiled weakly at Tamsin, and sat down in a beanbag. Tamsin flopped next to her, and Ivy and Nina sat opposite them. This time, Ivy and Nina didn't say anything. There was silence in the cubby house.

Casey bit her lip. She knew now that she had to make Tamsin understand why she had been so cross. It was a hard thing to explain, though. She just had to try to find the right words.

Casey stood up again and faced Tamsin. 'When I told you my secret,' she began slowly, 'it was like giving you a little piece of myself to take care of. I just thought . . . well, I expected you to understand that it was private.'

Casey paused for a moment while she thought about how to continue.

'I just think friends need to be able to trust each other with this kind of stuff,' she said eventually. 'I felt really sad and upset when you told the others, because it felt like you weren't looking after the piece of me that I'd given you.'

Casey stopped again, amazed that even the talkative Ivy was still quiet. She sat back down in the beanbag next to Tamsin.

Nina was nodding as though she understood. It definitely seemed as though everyone was really listening to what she had to say. And that felt good.

Casey felt a little worried she couldn't

see Tamsin's reaction, though. Tamsin was looking down at the floor.

'And besides,' Casey went on, 'I sort of freaked out that Dylan might find out. You know how when it gets out that you like someone, something changes between you? I really like Dylan as a friend. I don't want it to get all weird, like if he knows I like him . . . then we might act all goofy around each other.'

'Like getting all shaky when you're dishing out bolognaise sauce,' Ivy said with a little smile.

'Or walking straight into a pole when you're talking to someone in particular,' Nina added.

This time, Ivy and Nina both grinned. Ivy had whacked into a pole a week ago while she was talking to Adrian. Casey would have died of embarrassment if that had happened to her. But Ivy just thought it was funny, except for the bruise on her forehead!

Finally, Tamsin looked up. 'Yeah,' she said softly. 'That's true, I guess. It does get a bit strange when boys know you like them. But if you'd *explained* how you felt, I would have kept it a secret.' Tamsin's shoulders drooped a little. 'It was wrong of me to tell, though. I guess I made a mistake,' she finished quietly.

Casey bit her lip. Even though she was

glad they were talking, she was worried that Tamsin still looked unhappy.

And Casey knew deep down that there was something else she had to say to Tamsin. Because what Casey had done was way worse than making a mistake. She had deliberately tried to hurt Tamsin's feelings.

Casey had already forgiven Tamsin. But would Tamsin be able to forgive *her?*

Chapter Nine

Casey got up out of the beanbag and walked around the cubby. It felt as though there were so many words inside her that she had to stand up to give them more space.

'Tam,' she said, 'I, er, sometimes say things I don't mean when I'm angry.'

'That's true,' Ivy said. 'Like once, she told me I was never, ever going to be her —'

'*Everyone* says things they don't mean when they're angry,' Nina interrupted, giving Casey a supportive look, and Ivy a little pinch on the arm.

'Yeah, but maybe I'm a bit more like that than some people,' Casey admitted.

Casey noticed that Tamsin's eyebrows were raised, as though she wasn't quite sure what Casey was going to say next.

'When I said that thing about your dookie,' Casey said, 'I didn't actually mean it. I think your dookie is cute, Tam. And it was really, really mean of me to talk about it like that in front of everyone.'

Tamsin nodded, her face red. 'It *was* a bit embarrassing,' she said.

Casey sat down next to Tamsin again. 'I'm super, super sorry,' she said, feeling like she might cry. She so badly wanted Tamsin to forgive her.

Tamsin looked Casey directly in the eye. Then she grabbed her hand. 'It's OK,' she said kindly. 'Everyone makes mistakes.'

Casey felt as though a great weight had been lifted off her shoulders. She smiled at Tamsin gratefully. 'Thanks . . .' she began.

But Tamsin and Ivy and Nina weren't looking at her anymore. They were looking over at the window.

Casey heard a dull thud on the glass. Then she saw one red and one yellow snake, hanging down from the top of the window frame. They were held by a familiar hand.

'I think your brother might be out on the roof,' Tamsin grinned.

'I think my brother might be out of his mind,' Casey groaned.

'Out of his mind and out on the roof, with *our* snakes!' Ivy squealed.

Suddenly, the Secret Sisters were all scrambling out the door. Casey giggled as Nina grabbed one of Aaron's legs, and Ivy grabbed the other.

Casey grinned to herself as the girls pulled Aaron down onto the balcony of the cubby house.

It was great to see everyone acting like they were on the same team again. It was even better to watch them win back the red and yellow snakes!

'Hey, you guys *did* save us the red and

yellow ones,' Ivy giggled as Aaron climbed down, chuckling.

Casey looked at Tamsin slyly.

Tamsin winked at her, and said cheekily, 'As if we wouldn't save them for you! What sort of friends do you think we are?'

Chapter Ten

Casey smiled as she poured each of her friends a glass of lemonade. It was fantastic to have everything back to normal.

'Hey, let's do that quiz,' Nina suggested, flipping through Casey's magazine. 'It's called, *What sort of friend are you?* Is everybody ready?'

'Yep!' the others called out together.

'All right, question one,' Nina began.

1. Do you know your friends'
   favourite colours, movies,
   singers, and actors?

'Definitely!' they all yelled.

Nina laughed as she put each of their initials next to the A on the quiz sheet. They spent so much time talking about this stuff there was no way any of them would get *that* question wrong.

Nina moved on to question two.

2. Have you been on camps
   or holidays together?

'Well, that's easy,' Ivy said. 'We all went on the school camp together last term. Remember how Casey freaked out on the flying fox? And her face was all screwed up like this?'

Everyone cracked up as Ivy did a great impression of Casey on the flying fox.

Hey, I wasn't that bad!

'Yeah, and I also remember a certain person falling over face first in the mud on the obstacle course,' Casey snorted.

It was ages until they got to question three. But nobody cared. It was just great fun doing the quiz together!

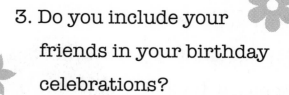

3. Do you include your friends in your birthday celebrations?

'Definitely,' Tamsin called out. Again, everybody agreed.

Nina was quiet for a moment as she studied the quiz page. Then she read out the next question.

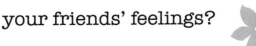

4. Do you always tell the truth, even if it might hurt your friends' feelings?

'Yes,' Ivy said. 'Of course it's yes.'

Casey watched as Nina shook her head. 'No way, Ives,' she objected. 'Like, some things you just shouldn't say.'

'Yeah,' Tamsin agreed with Nina. 'For example, if Ivy got a new top that she absolutely loved, and I absolutely hated, I'm not going to tell her that, am I? That would just be mean.'

'But if she asked your opinion,' Casey said, 'then you should tell her the truth. Don't you think?'

'Of course you shouldn't!' Nina and Tamsin said together.

'Of course you should!' Ivy and Casey countered.

'Shouldn't!' Nina and Tamsin giggled.

'Should!' Casey and Ivy yelled.

'Shouldn't!'

Suddenly, all the girls were up, dancing around and singing 'should' and 'shouldn't'. Ivy was the first to put her 'should' into a funny little shimmy as she danced around the cubby.

Soon, though, all the Secret Sisters were shimmying to their own chant.

Casey paused for a minute, and watched her dancing, disagreeing friends.

It didn't matter that they had different opinions. Maybe they all had different rules for what they should tell and what they should keep secret.

Maybe they all had different ideas of when they should tell the truth, or when they should keep something to themselves.

And really, Casey was glad. The ideas that made them different also made each of them special.

Real life, and real friendships, weren't as simple as choosing an A or a B, like in a quiz.

And Casey wouldn't change that. Not for anything in the world.